For my two daughters, Fern and Sofia,
with all my love - R.W.

For lovely little James - G.P-R

ORCHARD BOOKS
96 Leonard Street, London EC2A 4XD
Orchard Books Australia
32-45/51 Huntley Street, Alexandria NSW 2015
ISBN 1 84362 193 2
Text © Richard Waring 2003
Illustrations © Guy Parker-Rees 2003
The rights of Richard Waring to be identified as the author and
Guy Parker-Rees to be identified as the illustrator of this work has
been asserted by them in accordance with the Copyrights,
Designs and Patents Act, 1988.
A CIP catalogue record of this book is available from the British Library.
1 3 5 7 9 10 8 6 4 2
Printed in Singapore

Ducky Dives In!

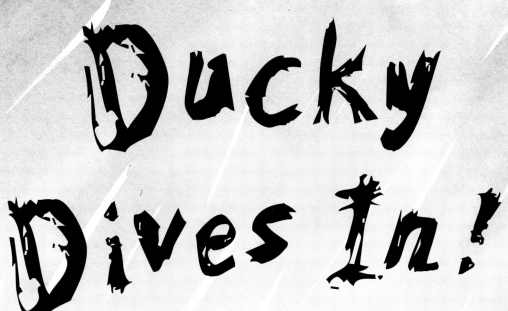

Richard Waring

Illustrated by Guy Parker-Rees

There was once a duck who loved to be mucky.
He loved puddles and anything…

sludgy,

squelchy,

and slushy.

The more he could splat,
the more he would quack...

and then quackle!

And cluckle...

and chuckle!

But whenever Mucky Ducky sneaked off to splash in the sloppy old sow trough, he would suddenly hear a very loud…

QUACK!

And there would stand Mummy Duck – and Mummy Duck would march him back to the big pond.

She would scrub him until he shone.
And as she scrubbed she would sing,

"A scrub-a-dub duck! For a good little duck
needs to be spotlessly clean!"

So whenever Mucky Ducky
was about to spring into
the slimy stream,

or the dirty puddle
in the pig-yard,

or lurk under
the leaking gutters
by the lambs' lean-tos…

...he would hear a

QUACK!

And there
would stand
Mummy Duck.

Mummy Duck always wanted him
to look smart and be squeaky-clean.

Now, behind the woodshed,
down a little path,
was an old millpond.

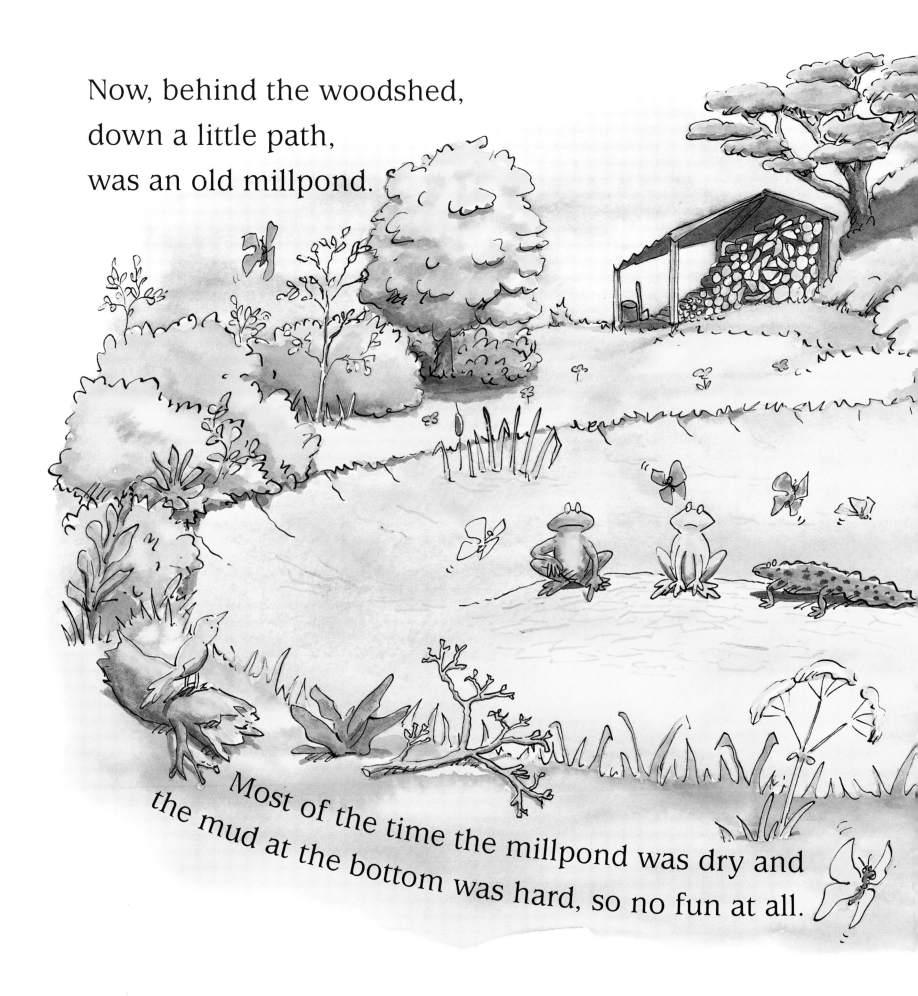

Most of the time the millpond was dry and
the mud at the bottom was hard, so no fun at all.

But when it rained, the hard mud turned superbly soft and sensationally sludgy.

And one day it rained…

...and rained...

and rained.

And Mucky Ducky schemed
and plotted and planned.

And waited…

While Mummy Duck was looking the
other way, Mucky Ducky slunk
silently up the side
of the bank.

Mummy Duck did not see him.

He sneaked through
the shrubbery,

and flitted past
the flower-beds.

And still Mummy Duck did not see him.

But as he crept through the clover patch, the tip of his shiny yellow tail waggled just above the grass. And Mummy Duck saw it…

and she wondered…

...and she looked up at the rain...

then down at the pond...

…and then she remembered the millpond…

and

Mucky Ducky!

And off Mummy Duck dashed.

She took a short cut right through the slimy stream,

She hurried under the leaking gutters by the lambs' lean-tos,

then pounded through the dirty puddle in the pig-yard.

and even over the muddy murky mere,

until finally Mummy Duck saw Mucky Ducky.

But Mucky Ducky had
almost reached the edge
of the millpond! Mummy Duck
sprinted as fast as possible towards the pond.

Mucky Ducky got **nearer** and **nearer** to the mud as Mummy Duck ran **faster** and **faster** and got **closer** and **closer**.

And just as Mummy Duck was about to reach out and grab Mucky Ducky…

...she slipped on her slimy, muddy foot and started to slide and slither

along the path...

...and splashed into the middle of the grubbiest, sludgiest, squelchiest pile of mud in the whole farm!

Mucky Ducky looked at Mummy Duck.
Mummy Duck looked at Mucky Ducky.

Mummy Duck said quack...

and then quackle!

And cluckle...

and chuckle!

squelched and slushed together, all day long.